Note to Parents

Reading books together can be one of the most pleasurable activities you share with your child. Young children love to spend time with their parents, and the opportunity to be the focus of your undivided attention. To get the most out of reading together, try to find a relaxed time that suits your family. Remember, reading should be fun, so show your enthusiasm and this will transfer to your child. If he or she is wriggling away, leave it for another occasion.

First Time Stories show familiar situations from everyday life that young children can relate to easily. Repetition helps children understand, so I suggest you read this book together more than once. You can use the story as a chance to talk about similar situations in your own child's life. As you read, follow the words with your finger to show the connection of the written word to what you are saying. Encourage your child's imagination if he or she wants to tell a different story from the pictures. Above all, enjoy reading together!

Eileen Hayes
Parenting Consultant to the NSPCC

Time to See the Doctor

Heather Maisner

ILLUSTRATED BY Kristina Stephenson

KINGFISHER

One warm day in spring, Mum asked, “Who wants to go to the zoo tomorrow?”

“Me,” said Amy. “I want to see the koalas.”

“Me,” said Ben. “I want to see the lions.”

“Me,” said Dad. “I want to see the cheetah. It’s the fastest animal on earth and it runs like this.”

He chased Amy and Ben round the garden, with Figaro the cat close behind.

That night, Ben dreamed he was a cheetah racing across the plains. But he woke up feeling hot and tired.

"It's because I was a cheetah," he told Amy.

At breakfast, Ben hardly touched his food and his eyes felt heavy. Dad took his temperature with a thermometer.

"We must take you to the doctor," he said. "But I want to go to the zoo," Ben moaned. "Doctor first," Dad insisted.

The doctor's surgery was crowded. A girl had her leg in plaster. A little boy coughed and sneezed. Amy and Ben played with the toys. Ben pushed a truck slowly round the room. His head throbbed and his ears ached.

"I want to go home," he mumbled.

"It will be your turn soon," said Dad, lifting him onto his lap.

"But I don't want to see the doctor," Ben whispered. "It might hurt."

The receptionist called Ben's name and they walked to the doctor's roon It had a desk and a tall bed covered with white paper.

I don't want to go to bed here, Ben thought, clinging tightly to Dad. *I want to go home.*

The doctor said, “Hello, Ben,
I hear you’re not feeling very well.”
Ben turned his face away.

"Can you open your mouth wide and say 'Aah' so that I can check your throat?" the doctor asked. Ben shook his head. He didn't want to open his mouth.

"How about letting me have a look at your ears?" said the doctor, but Ben buried his head in Dad's jacket, hiding his ears completely.

"Could you lift up your top, please, so that I can listen to your chest?" said the doctor. Ben shook his head and pulled his top down tight.

"I know," said Amy. "You can look at me instead."

Amy opened her mouth and said, "Aah", as the doctor looked at her throat.

"That tickles," she said with a giggle, as the doctor shone a light in her ears.

"That feels cold." Amy shivered as the doctor listened to her chest with the stethoscope.

Ben sat very still, watching out of the corner of his eye. But he sat up very straight when the doctor handed Amy a box of stickers. She chose one with a picture of a parrot. It said, "I am a brave girl."

“Can I have one too?”
Ben asked.
“Yes,” said the doctor.
“After I’ve examined you.”

Ben opened his mouth and said, “Aah”, just like Amy had done.

“That tickles,” he said as the doctor shone a light in his ears.

And the stethoscope was cold on his chest, just like Amy had said. But it didn't hurt at all.

“Don’t worry, Ben. You’ve got an ear infection,” the doctor said. “I’ll give your dad a prescription. You can take it to the chemist to get some medicine. It will make you feel much better.”

The doctor typed on her computer and handed the printed sheet to Dad.

“Now you can choose a sticker,” she told Ben. He chose one with a picture of a lion. It said, “I am a brave boy.”

On the way home, they stopped at the chemist's. The shelves were filled with bottles and pills and all sorts of things for the bathroom.

Ben rubbed his forehead and pressed his ear.

"It's all right," Amy whispered. "I've had earache, too. It hurts, but it goes away."

Dad gave the prescription
to the chemist. A little while later,
she handed him the medicine for Ben.

At home, Ben told Mum, "I'm a brave boy."

"Of course you are," she said, cuddling him close and carrying him upstairs to his room. She gave him a spoonful of medicine and wiped his face gently.

As Ben slid down under the sheets, with Figaro beside him, he looked at his sticker and asked, "Are real lions brave like me?"

"I don't know," Mum replied. "But as soon as you're better, we'll go to the zoo to find out."

The publisher thanks Eileen Hayes, Parenting Advisor to the NSPCC, Dr. Dawn Peters and Dr. John-Paul Westwood for their kind assistance in the development of this book.

For the children of Flora Gardens School, Hammersmith – H.M.
For Nigel – K.S.

KINGFISHER
An imprint of Kingfisher Publications Plc
New Penderel House, 283-288 High Holborn
London WC1V 7HZ
www.kingfisherpub.com

First published by Kingfisher 2004
2 4 6 8 10 9 7 5 3 1

A CIP catalogue record for this book is available from the British Library.

ISBN 0 7534 0995 X

Printed in Singapore
1TR/0704/TWP/PICA(PICA)/150MA